Go to Sleep, Little Farm

For my mother, who read me across the threshold of night, as the ordinary turned into story, and story into dream. —M.L.R.

To Abigail and Bella, who are forever in my dreams. —C.S.N.

Text copyright © 2014 by Mary Lyn Ray

Illustrations copyright © 2014 by Christopher Silas Neal

www.hmhco.com

The text of this book was set in Century Schoolbook.

The illustrations were rendered in mixed media.

Library of Congress Cataloging-in-Publication Control Number 2013036936

ISBN 978-0-544-15014-0

Manufactured in China

SCP 10 9 8 7 6 5 4 3

4500519864

Go to Sleep, Little Farm

By Mary Lyn Ray

with art by Christopher Silas Neal

HOUGHTON MIFFLIN HARCOURT
Boston   New York

Somewhere a bee

makes a bed in a rose,
because the bee knows day has
come to a close.

Somewhere a beaver weaves a bed in a bog.

Somewhere a bear

finds a bed in a log.

Somewhere gray mice hide their bed under roots,

safe from the owl who *whoo-whoo-hoot*s.

Somewhere a fox calls her pups to their den—

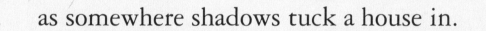

as somewhere shadows tuck a house in.

Cows and horses on the hill hear their pasture grow more still.

Chickens roost where chickens will

Now that the day and the sun have gone,
quiet spreads and evening comes on—
speckled with stars like the spots on a fawn.

And somewhere someone yawns a small yawn.

Already, trees sleep the way that trees sleep.

Brown rabbits snuggle in a sleepy rabbit heap.

All around, dusk turns to night.

Time for a father to turn off the light.

Now little fish lie still in a brook.

Somewhere a story goes to sleep in a book.

Somewhere a worm sleeps in the dirt.

Somewhere a pocket sleeps in a skirt.

Even small breezes sleep in the skies.

And somewhere a mother says, "Close your eyes."

Then somewhere a secret curls in an ear,

just as dreams flicker near . . .

some for each rabbit,

each mouse,

and each fox,

some for the minutes that sleep inside clocks,

2

some for the slippers asleep on a rug,

and some for someone who gets one more hug.

Now is the dark time. Now night has come.
Now is the time that dreams bloom from.

So go to sleep, little fish.
Go to sleep, little farm. Go to sleep,
woolly sheep,
back in the barn.

Go to sleep, beaver.

Go to sleep, little deer.

Quiet is the night now.

Go to sleep, little ear.